DISNEP

BAMBI

Ladybird Books

One day, as the sun rose, there was great excitement in the forest. A new prince had been born. It was a little fawn, son of the great stag, Prince of the Forest.

Bambi's first great friend was Thumper the rabbit, who showed the little fawn the world of the forest. Forest life could be fun – but sometimes it could be cruel as well...

A catalogue record for this book is available from the British Library.

Published by Ladybird Books Ltd Loughborough Leicestershire UK

Printed in England (7)

All the animals and birds came to welcome him. The fawn opened his eyes to see happy faces all round him.

For a moment the fawn looked
frightened. Then he got to his feet.
At first his thin legs trembled, but
soon he stood firm and strong.

A young rabbit asked, "What is his name?"

"Bambi," answered the mother deer.

"That's nice," said the rabbit. "*My* name's Thumper." And he hopped away to spread the news about the new fawn.

It was summertime, and the forest was beautiful, with flowers all around. Bambi loved to walk with his mother along the leafy paths, finding new surprises every day.

Once he saw some opossums hanging upside down. Another time, he found a mother quail with her nine babies beside her.

Sometimes Bambi played with Thumper the rabbit, who showed him all sorts of new things and told him their names.

"Those are birds," said Thumper – and Bambi said, "Birds," after him. It was his very first word.

Then a butterfly came along.
"Bird," said Bambi.

"No, that's a butterfly," said
Thumper, laughing.

Bambi bent his head to smell some
flowers.

"Butterfly," he said, trying out his
new word.

"No," said Thumper. "They're
flowers."

Suddenly a small black pointed nose poked up out of the flowers.

"Flower?" asked Bambi.

"No, no," laughed Thumper. "That's a skunk."

"He can call me Flower if he wants to," said the skunk. Bambi had found another new friend!

One morning Bambi's mother took him to the meadow. He had never been there before, and it was a wonderful place to play. He was racing up and down when he saw another little fawn nearby.

Bambi was so surprised that he bounded away up the meadow, pretending not to see her.

"Don't be shy, Bambi," called his mother. "Come and meet Faline. She's your cousin."

Soon Faline and Bambi were playing happily together, chasing each other round the little hillocks.

Then came the sound of running feet, and the stags burst out of the woods. They were calling, "Danger – MAN!" as they ran.

All the birds and animals hurried into the trees, and in a moment the meadow was empty.

Bambi and his mother hid in their thicket, and trembled with fear as they heard shouts and loud roaring noises quite close by.

"That was MAN, Bambi," explained his mother. "He carries a long stick called a gun that can kill you. He means DANGER to all of us here in the forest."

Summer passed and the weather
grew colder. Bambi woke up one
day shivering, to find that the
world had turned white in the
night. Every blade of grass was
covered with a white coat, and so
was every tree and every bush.

His mother was watching him.
"That's snow, Bambi," she said.

Bambi put one hoof out onto the snow to feel the cold crispness. Then he walked forward carefully, lifting his feet high. It was a lovely winter's day and the sun sparkled on the snow.

In the distance, Bambi was surprised to see Thumper playing on *top* of the pond! He hurried towards his friend and skidded on the smooth ice. Down he fell!

Thumper just laughed at him!

Soon Bambi could walk without
slipping, and he and Thumper had
a fine time playing in the snow.

Once they heard a faint snore from a snowbank. They looked down a deep burrow and saw the little skunk there, fast asleep.

"Let's wake him up," said Bambi.

"No," said Thumper. "Skunks always sleep right through the winter. It's called hibernating."

Winter was fun at first, but as time
went on, there was less and less
food. All the animals grew hungry.
Sometimes there was nothing at all
for Bambi and his mother to eat,
except the bark from trees.

Then one day there was a change in the air. It was a little warmer, and Bambi's mother found some new green grass under the snow.

Bambi and his mother were eating the grass hungrily when suddenly there was a loud BANG not far off. "Run, Bambi," said his mother. "Run as quickly as you can, and don't look back."

Bambi ran and ran, his mother just behind him. Then there was another loud BANG. Bambi ran faster than ever.

When at last he stopped, his sides
heaving, his mother was nowhere
to be seen. The forest was quiet.

Bambi looked all round, then began to call wildly for his mother. In a moment the great Prince of the Forest came to his side.

"Your mother can never be with you again," he said quietly. "Now you must be brave and learn to walk alone."

The long winter was over. There
were flowers here and there, and
the trees were tipped with leaves
and buds. The spring sun shone on
Bambi's coat as he walked along
the forest path. He carried his head
proudly, for now he had a fine set
of antlers.

Suddenly he found another deer
beside him – a beautiful doe. "Do
you remember me, Bambi?" she
asked. "I'm Faline."

And after a moment, they went on
down the path together.

"Not so fast!" said a deep voice.
"Faline is going with me."

It was a deer called Ronno, his
antlers lowered ready for battle.

Bambi had never fought before, but he wasted no time. He charged straight at Ronno and they met with a crash. They fought fiercely, but at last one of Ronno's antlers broke. Then Bambi managed to wound Ronno in the shoulder.

Beaten at last, Ronno limped off
into the forest. Faline came back to
Bambi's side and they walked away
through the trees to the meadow,
to start their life together.

Summer passed happily for Bambi
and Faline.

Then one autumn day Bambi and
the great stag heard dogs barking
and smelled MAN. "Yes," the
great stag said, "it *is* MAN, with
tents and campfires. We will have
to go to the hills."

As Bambi called Faline, the dogs came close. He lowered his antlers and held them off, calling, "Hurry, Faline." But when he turned to run, there was a loud BANG. A dreadful pain went through Bambi, but it didn't stop him.

The great stag ran at his side, saying, "The forest is on fire from the campfires. We must make for the river."

They rushed through the fire, through the cool water of the river and onto the far shore. Many other animals had already reached safety there.

Faline was there too and she gently licked Bambi's wounded shoulder.

There was a long cold winter to live through in the fire-blackened forest. Then came spring. New leaves and grass and flowers grew where the fire had been, and the forest was beautiful once more.

And soon news went round the forest that Faline had had *two* babies. Squirrels and birds and rabbits came to see them.

Not far away the proud father
watched over them all – Bambi,
the new great Prince of the Forest.